KV-245-020

3

The children laughed at me.

28 OCT 2023

2 1 MAR 2054

READING CHAMPION

Show Time

WITHDRAWN FROM BROMLEY LIBRARIES

by Jackie Walter and Ivan Barrera

WITHDRAWN FROM BROMLEY LIBRARIES

Bromley Libraries

30128 80538 005 5

I put on my trousers.

I put on my shoes.

The children laughed at me.

I put on my coat.

The children laughed at me.

I put on my hat.

The children laughed at me.

I put on my flower.

19

Story trail

Start at the beginning of the story trail. Ask your child to retell the story in their own words, pointing to each picture in turn to recall the sequence of events.

Start

Independent Reading

This series is designed to provide an opportunity for your child to read on their own. These notes are written for you to help your child choose a book and to read it independently.

In school, your child's teacher will often be using reading books which have been banded to support the process of learning to read. Use the book band colour your child is reading in school to help you make a good choice. *Show Time* is a good choice for children reading at Pink 1B in their classroom to read independently.

The aim of independent reading is to read this book with ease, so that your child enjoys the story and relates it to their own experiences.

About the book

In this story, a clown makes the children laugh at him with his clothes and props, until he decides to have the last laugh!

Before reading

Help your child to learn how to make good choices by asking: "Why did you choose this book? Why do you think you will enjoy it?" Support your child to think about what they already know about the story context. Look at the cover together and ask: "What do you think the story will be about?" Read the title aloud and ask: "Who do you think is going to be the main character in the story?"

Remind your child that they can try to sound out the letters to make a word if they get stuck.

Decide together whether your child will read the story independently or read it aloud to you. When books are short, as at Pink 1B, your child may wish to do both!

During reading

If reading aloud, support your child if they hesitate or ask for help by telling the word. Remind your child of what they know and what they can do independently.

If reading to themselves, remind your child that they can come and ask for your help if stuck.

After reading:

Use the story trail to encourage your child to retell the story in the right sequence, in their own words.

Support comprehension by asking your child to tell you about the story. Help your child think about the messages in the book that go beyond the story. Ask: "Do you think the clown wanted to make the children laugh? What did the clown do differently at the end?"

Give your child a chance to respond to the story: "Did you have a favourite part? If you saw a clown, what could they do to make you laugh?"

Extending learning

Help your child extend the story structure by using the same sentence pattern and adding some more elements: "There might be other items the clown could put on to make the children laugh. What items can you think of?"

On a few of the pages, check your child can finger point accurately by asking them to show you how they kept their place in the print by tracking from word to word.

Help your child to use letter information by asking them to find the interest word on each page by using the first letter. For example: "Which word is 'hat'? How do you know it is that word?"

Franklin Watts
First published in Great Britain in 2022 by Hodder and Stoughton
Copyright © Hodder and Stoughton Ltd, 2022

All rights reserved.

Series Editors: Jackie Hamley and Melanie Palmer
Series Advisors and Development Editors: Dr Sue Bodman and Glen Franklin
Series Designers: Cathryn Gilbert and Peter Scoulding

A CIP catalogue record for this book is
available from the British Library.

ISBN 978 1 4451 7431 0 (hbk)
ISBN 978 1 4451 7432 7 (pbk)
ISBN 978 1 4451 8547 7 (ebook)

Printed in China

Franklin Watts
An imprint of
Hachette Children's Group
Part of Hodder and Stoughton
Carmelite House
50 Victoria Embankment
London EC4Y 0DZ

An Hachette UK Company
www.hachette.co.uk

www.franklinwatts.co.uk

FSC
www.fsc.org
MIX
Paper from
responsible sources
FSC® C104740